A ROOKIE READER®

OH NO, OTIS!

By Julie E. Frankel

Illustrated by Clovis Martin

Prepared under the direction of Robert Hillerich, Ph.D.

CHILDREN'S PRESS
A Division of Grolier Publishing
Sherman Turnpike
Danbury, Connecticut 06816

Library of Congress Cataloging-in-Publication Data

Frankel, Julie E.
    Oh no, Otis! / by Julie E. Frankel ; illustrated by
Clovis Martin.
       p.   cm. — (A Rookie reader)
    Summary: A two-year-old boy gets into and opens
everything except the birthday present that his parents
want him to open.
    ISBN 0-516-02009-9
    [1. Behavior—Fiction. 2. Birthdays—Fiction.
3. Stories in rhyme.] I. Martin, Clovis, ill. II. Title.
III. Series.
PZ8.3.F84798Oh   1991
[E]—dc20
                            91-15328
                               CIP
                                AC

Oh no, Otis! Don't open that!

4

Oh, Otis, now look at the cat!

Otis! Otis! Don't play in there!

Oh, Otis, now look at your hair!

10

Otis! No! Don't pull on that!

Oh, Otis, now look at the mat!

14

Oh no, Otis! Don't put
that on your face!

Oh, Otis, now look at this place!

17

18

Oh, Otis!

What am I going to do with you?

Surprise, Otis!
And Happy Birthday, too!

FOR OTIS

21

22

Okay, Otis . . . now
you may open this.

24

Yes, this is for you.

Otis? Otis?

Oh no! Now what did you do?

Oh, Otis!
We love you!

WORD LIST

am	hair	oh	the
and	happy	okay	there
at	I	on	this
birthday	in	open	to
cat	is	Otis	too
did	look	place	we
do	love	play	what
don't	mat	pull	with
face	may	put	yes
for	no	surprise	you
going	now	that	your